A Lil' DIRT Between My TOES

Kyndra Ray

Illustrated by Alice Wong

To: Rivers

Kyndra Ray

ISBN: 978-0-9960506-0-9

Edited by: Jessica Carelock and Amy Ashby

Published by Warren Publishing
Charlotte, NC
www.warrenpublishing.net
Printed in the United States

I am thankful to God for the amazing
blessings in my life and to Dimples.

"The LORD is gracious and full of compassion,
Slow to anger and great in mercy."

-PSALM 145:8

Dec. 25, 2018

To, ~~Esta~~ Rivers,
Always let "Christ" be your
guiding Light in your life!
Merry Christmas! God Bless!

Love. Uncle Chuck
aunt Myra & Kyle

I have a lil' dirt between my toes.
I scrubbed last night from feet to nose.
Plain ol' soap and water, then I'm good to go,
But sometimes, I still have a lil' dirt between my toes.

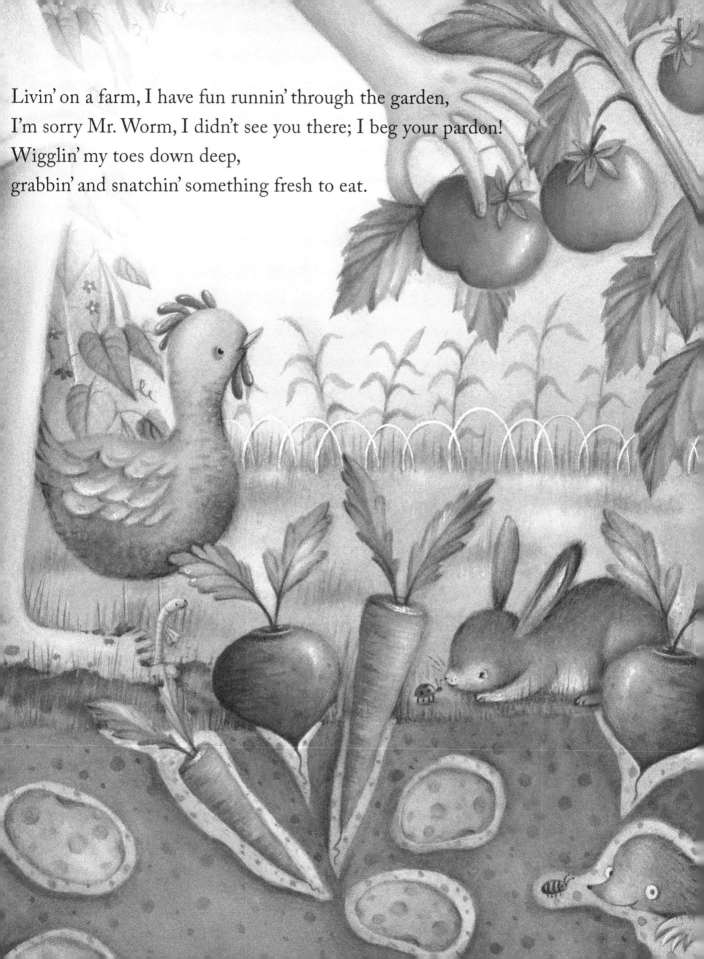

Livin' on a farm, I have fun runnin' through the garden,
I'm sorry Mr. Worm, I didn't see you there; I beg your pardon!
Wigglin' my toes down deep,
grabbin' and snatchin' something fresh to eat.

Grandma hollers, I've stepped on her beets.
"Lordy child, look at your feet!"
I scrubbed last night, I promise I did.
I just can't help it, I'm bein' a kid!

Cows are bawlin', Grandpa's callin',
"Time to eat, I've got a sweet treat."
I pick up both feet, runnin' and hollerin',
"Grandpa, I'm comin'," past the pigs a'wallerin'.

Standin' on that ol' fence line, tossin' corn husks,
I still have hours and hours to play before dusk.

Well, what do you know?
Even the cows have a lil' dirt between their toes!
Steamin' patties fill the field by my side,
I wonder if that bull will ever let me ride?

The challenge I set for myself today,
is to see how high I can climb the hay.
Wibbly wobbly, I'm almost there.
Here comes Grandpa; better get out of here!

What's that I hear? Dad's in the field cuttin' hay.
I hop on the fence, hopin' to catch a ride for the day.
There's always work on the farm, but then I get to play.
I find dirt between my toes, but I think it's okay.

Time for something new. Oh, what to do?
Maybe I'll play with my sisters,
they're runnin' barefoot too.
Let's climb a tree, play hide and seek,

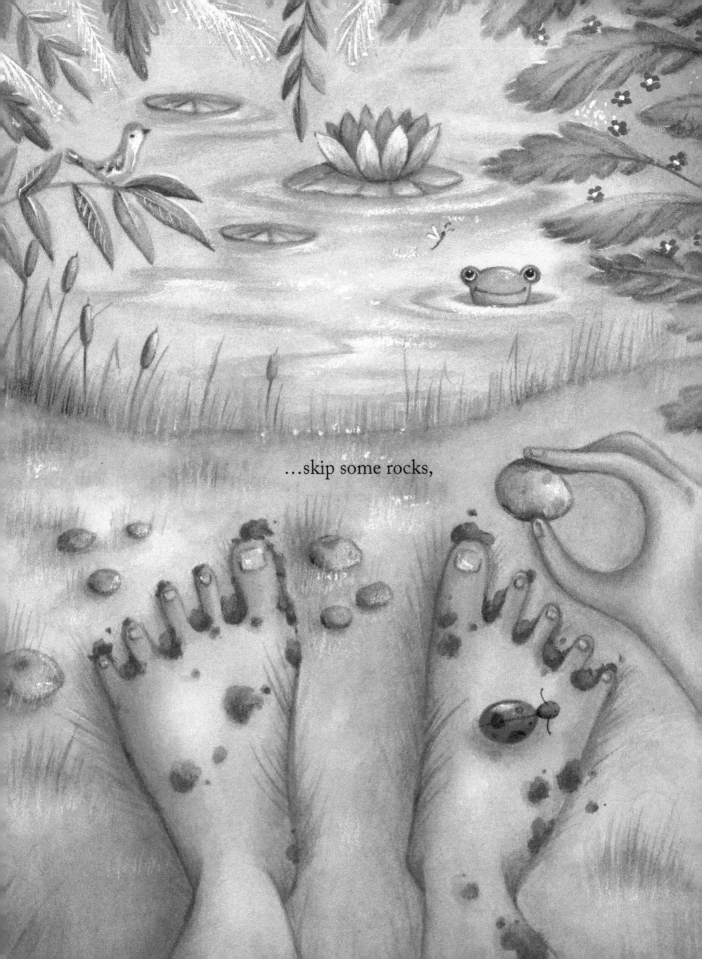

...skip some rocks,

...then grab somethin' cold to drink.

Oh, to feel the soft summer wind.
The day is almost at an end.
My belly starts to grumble, then I feel a rumble,
I'm hungry after a day of runnin' and tumbles.

I holler, "Mama, I'm on my way!"
as I hurdle over a bale of hay.
I get to the house, oh what a nice surprise,
dinner tonight is gonna be outside.

I go wash my hands, and clean off my face.
Now it's time for us to say grace.
We all gather 'round, ready to eat.
Mama's fixed for us a sweet lil' treat.

...esh peaches galore,
...but wait, there's more!

Fried chicken,
fresh beans,
and corn on the cob,
all out of our garden,
vegetables by the gob.

The summer sun begins to set,
This was a day of fun—no regrets.

Mama says, "Bath time! Go scrub, and then bed!"
"Don't forget the dirt between your toes!" Grandma says.

I'm tucked in bed after a long day of play,
Staring up at the moon, I'll wrap up my day.
Now the light has gone away,
until tomorrow comes our way.
One big yawn as my eyes begin to close.
Even in my dreams, there's a lil' dirt between my toes.

Dear Lord, please listen while I pray,
thank you for this adventurous day.

All these memories I'll forever keep,
of playin' on the farm in my bare feet.

Please keep me safe as I sleep,
so I can wake tomorrow and
chase the sheep!

CPSIA information can be obtained
at www.ICGtesting.com
Printed in the USA
LVHW07*2140270918
591611LV00006B/10/P